Marie Hamilton

A Garland of Old Historical Ballads 1600-1752

Marie Hamilton

A Garland of Old Historical Ballads 1600-1752

ISBN/EAN: 9783744787864

Printed in Europe, USA, Canada, Australia, Japan

Cover: Foto ©Andreas Hilbeck / pixelio.de

More available books at **www.hansebooks.com**

"INVENIRE."

A Garland of Old Historical Ballads.

1600-1732.

I.
Marie Hamilton.

II.
Rob Oig.

III.
Willy and Mary.

" You, O Books, are the golden vessels of the Temple ; burning lights to be ever held in the hand."

RICHARD AUNGERVYLE.

PRIVATELY PRINTED FOR THE AUNGERVYLE SOCIETY,
EDINBURGH.

1881.

INTRODUCTION.

ALTHOUGH fragmentary or mutilated editions of the three following ballads have appeared, still for practical purposes they may be considered as unedited to the present day, for the variations are so extensive, and the fragments so small a part of the whole, as to be quite unworthy the attention of the literary scholar. The third ballad especially is unknown, no copy, so far as I have been able to ascertain, being in any library in the kingdom. It is hoped that the particulars given in the introduction to the second ballad will be found interesting, relating as they do to a curious episode in the career of a son of the celebrated Rob Roy. The well known ballad of Marie Hamilton, which has partly appeared in so many collections, is now, I believe, first printed in its entirety.

MARIE HAMILTON.

THIS very curious version of the well known ballad was taken down early in the present century from the lips of an old lady in Annandale. It is not, perhaps, so perfect in form as that published by Sir Walter Scott in his Border Minstrelsy, but we strongly suspect that the owner of Abbotsford was much given to "improving" those ballads which he did so much to revive the popularity of. C. K. Sharpe, the Editor of "A Ballad Book," has given a very mutilated edition of this ballad. In his introduction he tells us :—

"It is singular that, during the reign of the Czar Peter, one of his Empress's attendants, a Miss Hamilton, was executed for the murder of a natural child, not her first crime in that way, as was suspected ; and the Emperor, whose admiration of her beauty did not preserve her life, stood upon the scaffold until her head was struck off, which he lifted by the ear, and kissed on the lips."

This story must evidently have got confused with that of Marie Hamilton, one of the "Queen's Maries," for it is not likely that if Marie Hamilton was executed in Edinburgh, her parents should have resided across the sea, as stated in verses 19 to 22 in this ballad.

Marie Hamilton.

I.

"This nicht the Queen has four Maries,
  "Each fair as fair can be,
"There's Marie Seton, and Marie Beaton,
  "And Marie Carmichael and me."

II.

Word's gane to the kitchen,
　　And word's gane to the ha',
That Marie Hamilton gangs wi' bairn,
　　To the hichest Stewart of a'.

III.

He's courted her in the kitchen,
　　He's courted her in the ha'
He's courted her in the laigh cellar,
　　And that was worst of a'.

IV.

The bairn's tyed in her apron,
　　And thrown intill the sea,
" O sink ye, swim ye, bonnie wee babe,
　　" You'l ne'er get mair o' me."

V.

" Oh I have born this bonnie wee babe
　　" Wi' mickle toil and pain ;
" Gae hame, gae hame, you bonnie wee babe,
　　" For nurse I dare be nane."

VI.

Then doun cam Queen Marie,
　　Goud tassels tying her hair,
Saying, " Marie Mild, where is the babe,
　　That I heard greet sae sair ? "

VII.

" There was nae babe intill my room,
　　" There was na habe wi' me ;
" It was but a touch o' a sair cholic
　　" Come o'er my fair bodie."

VIII.

The Queen turned down the blankets fine,
    Likewise the snae-white sheet,
And what she saw caused her many a tear,
    And made her sair to greet.

IX.

" O cruel mither," said the Queen,
    " A fiend possessed thee,
" But I will hang thee for this deed,
    " My Marie though thou be.

X.

" O, Marie, put on your robes o' black,
    " Or else your robes o' brown,
" For ye maun gang wi' me the nicht,
    " To see fair Edinbro' town."

XI.

" I winna' put on my robes o' black,
    " Nor yet my robes o' brown,
" But I'll put on my robes o' white,
    " To shine thro' Edinbro' town."

XII.

And some they mounted the black steed,
    And some mounted the brown,
But Marie mounted her milk-white steed,
    And rode foremost thro' the town.

XIII.

When she gaed up the Cannongate,
    She laugh'd loud laughters three ;
But when she cam doun the Cannongate,
    The tear blinded her e'e.

XIV.

When she gaed up the Parliament stair,
    The heel cam aff her shee,
And lang e'er she cam doon again,
    She was condemn'd to dee.

XV.

When she cam doon the Cannongate,
    The Cannongate sae free,
Mony a ladie looked o'er her window,
    Weeping for this ladie.

XVI.

" Ye need nae weep for me," she says,
    " Ye need nae weep for me,
" For had I not slain mine own sweet babe,
    " This death I wadna' dee.

XVII.

" Bring me a bottle of wine, she says,
    " The best that e'er ye hae,
" That I may drink to my weil wishers,
    " And they may drink to me.

XVIII.

" Yestreen the Queen had four Maries,
    " The nicht she'll hae but three,
" There was Marie Seton, and Marie Beaton,
    " And Marie Carmichael and me.

XIX

Ye mariners, ye mariners,
    That sail upon the see,
L   not my father or mother wit,
    The death that I maun dee.

XX.

" I was my parent's only hope,
    " They ne'er had ane but me,
" They little thought when I left hame,
    " They should nae mair me see."

XXI.

" Oh little did my mother think,
    " The day she cradled me,
" What lands I was to travel through,
    " What death I was to dee.

XXII.

" Oh, little did my father think,
    " The day he held up me,
" What lands I was to travel through,
    " What death I was to dee.

XXIII.

" Last nicht there were four Maries,
    " The nicht there'l be but three,
" There was Marie Seton, and Marie Beaton,
    " And Marie Carmichael and me "

ROB OIG.

THE manuscript of the following ballad was in the possession of the late James Maidment, Esq., Advocate, of Edinburgh, the contemporary and friend of Sir Walter Scott, Motherwell, &c. It bears internal evidence of having been written soon after the date of the event which it celebrates, notwithstanding one glaring blunder to which attention is drawn in a foot-note.

The Rob Oig alluded to is Robert M'Gregor, son of the celebrated Rob Roy. The victim of the crime was Jean Key, widow of James Key of Edinbelly.

James and Rob Oig M'Gregor were brought before the High Court of Justiciary charged with hamesucken, forcible abduction, and forcible marriage. James was seized first, and it was not till after his trial was concluded that Rob was apprehended and brought to justice. James's trial took place on July 13th, 1752. The indictment, which is of considerable interest, was in the following terms:—"That whereas, by the laws of God and of this and all other well governed realms, Hamesucken, or the violent entering into any person's house without licence, or contrary to the King's peace, or seeking or assaulting him or her there, where he or she was dwelling at the time, lying and rising nightly and daily, especially when that is done against a woman, or minor, a widow lately become such, and an heiress, with intent to do her a most heinous and atrocious injury. As also, the ravishing of women, or the forcible abduction, or violent carrying a woman from one place to another with intent either to violate her person against her will, or to force her to a marriage, or the causing a marriage, or the form thereof, forcibly and by concussion to be celebrated as betwixt a man and a woman; and, under pretence of such forced marriage, the violating her person without the free consent, and against the will of such woman, especially when such woman was a minor, an heiress, and lately become a widow; and when the man so forced upon her for a pretended husband, and who afterwards violated her person upon that pretence, was of a character, circumstance, and situation, utterly unbecoming or unfit for her, as being destitute of fortune, substance, or good fame, and reputed guilty of, or outlawed for, the most heinous crimes ; are all, and each of them, crimes of the most atrocious, shocking, and most detestable nature, and most severely punishable. Yet true it is, and of verity, that he the same James Drummond, had presumed to commit, and was guilty, actor, art and part, of all and every, or one or other of the aforesaid crimes, aggravated as aforesaid, in so far as, upon the 8th day of December 1750 years, in the evening thereof, under cloud and silence of night, or upon one or other of the days of the said month of December, or of the month of November immediately preceding, or of the month of January immediately following, Jean Key, daughter and sole heiress of the deceased James Key, portioner of Edinbelly, and relict of John Wright, lawful son of John Wright of Easter Glins, who had died in the month of October preceding, leaving the said Jean Key his widow, then a minor, going in the 19th year of her age, was then living at her own house at Edinbelly, in the parish of Balfron, and shire of Stirling, where she was lying and rising nightly and daily, under the protection of Almighty God, and of his Majesty's laws, and had then with her in her house, Janet Mitchell her mother, and Thomas Key, tenant in Boquhan, or Balquhan, her uncle or father's brother, and Annabell Mitchell, relict of John Fairlie, her aunt, or mother's sister, with servants and other members of the family, and then and there the said house was beset, invaded, and violently entered by a crew of lawless ruffians, armed with guns, swords, durks, pistols, or other warlike weapons ; amongst whom was he, the said James M'Gregor, *alias* Drummond, *alias* James Moore ; and Robert M'Gregor, *alias* Campbell, *alias* Drummond, *alias* Robert Oig ; and Ronald M'Gregor, *alias* Campbell, *alias* Drummond ; all three sons of the deceased Robert M'Gregor, commonly called and known by the name of Rob Roy ; and which Robert, brother to the said James Drummond, at that time stood declared an outlaw and fugitive from the laws, by a sentence of fugitation pronounced against him by the High Court of Justiciary, upon the 16th day of July, 1736, for not appearing to underly the law for the murder of John M'Claren of Wester Innernenty, in the parish of Balquhidder, and shire of

Perth: And the said James Drummond, and his said two brothers, were then and there accompanied by Duncan M'Gregor, *alias* Drummond, in Strathyre, and then prisoner in the Tolbooth of Edinburgh, and a number of other persons, armed as aforesaid, his accomplices in a most lawless, barbarous, and wicked enterprise, to attack and invade the said Jean Key in her own house, and violently and forcibly to carry her away from the same, in order to compel her to be married to the said Robert M'Gregor, *alias* Campbell, *alias* Drummond, *alias* Robert Oig, brother to the said James; and in prosecution of the said wicked design, he the said James M'Gregor, *alias* Drummond, *alias* James Moore, with his accomplices, and armed as aforesaid, came at the time and place foresaid, to the house of the said Jean Key, and having placed guards at the doors and windows of the said house, in order to prevent the said Jean Key from escaping, or any assistance being brought to her, he, the said James, and the said Robert and Ronald, brothers to the said James, and others of his accomplices, did violently and forcibly enter the house of the said Jean Key, and not finding her in the room where the said James first entered, he, or some other of his accomplices, did, with many horrid oaths and imprecations, threaten to murder every person in the family, or to burn the house and every person in it alive, unless the said Jean Key should instantly be produced to him, which obliged the said Janet Mitchell, her mother, to bring her out of a closet to which she had retired in great fear and terror in order to conceal herself, and that as soon as she was brought into the presence of the said invaders, he, the said James M'Gregor, in a daring and violent manner, told her, that he and his accomplices were come there in order to marry her to the said Robert, his brother. And upon her desiring to be allowed till next morning, or some few hours, to deliberate upon the answer she was to give to so unexpected and sudden a proposal as a marriage betwixt her, then not two months a widow, and a man with whom she had no manner of acquaintance, after some further discourse or expostulation, he, the said James M'Gregor, or one or other of his accomplices, laid violent hands upon the said Jean Key, within her own dwelling house as aforesaid, and in a most barbarous, cruel, and most unbecoming and indecent manner, dragged her to the door, while she was making all the resistance in her power, and crying out for help and assistance, and uttering many bitter lamentations, and after she was thus dragged to the door, the said James M'Gregor, or one or other of his accomplices, did, with force and violence, most barbarously and inhumanly lay the said Jean Key upon a horse, on which the said Robert M'Gregor, or one or other of his company, was mounted, placing her body across the horse upon the fore, or fore part of the saddle, after having tied her arms with ropes, and during all the time these horrid and barbarous outrages were acting, he, the said James M'Gregor and his accomplices, or one or other of them, did threaten, with execrable oaths, immediately to murder any person who should offer to give the said Jean Key the least assistance, and after having posted some of their number with their arms, as guards upon the said Jean Key's house, to remain for some time to prevent any persons coming out to alarm the neighbourhood, and procure assistance to rescue the said Jean Key, the said James M'Gregor and his accomplices, or some or other of them, did, in a violent, barbarous, and cruel manner, carry off the said Jean Key from her own dwelling house, as aforesaid, lying across the fore part of the saddle, with her arms tied, while she was crying out for help and assistance, and making many bitter lamentations to the house of John Leckie, maltman and brewer at the Kirk of Buchanan, about six miles distant from Edinbelly, where the said Jean Key continued to give all evidences in her power of the deepest grief and sorrow for her unhappy fate, and from thence, in a few hours, the said James M'Gregor and his accomplices carried her by force and violence to a place called Rueindennan and from thence by water to some part of the Highlands, about the upper part of Lochlomond, out of the reach of her friends and relations, where she was detained in captivity, and carried from place to place for upwards of three months, and during this captivity, whilst her person and life were in the power of the said James M'Gregor or his accomplices, he and they, or some or other of them, in further prosecution of the wicked purpose for which they were guilty of the hamesucken and violent abduction aforesaid, caused to be celebrated the form of a pretented marriage betwixt him the said Robert M'Gregor, *alias* Campbell, *alias* Drummond, *alias* Robert Oig. brother to the said James M'Gregor, and outlaw and fugitive for murder as aforesaid, and they, without the free consent and against the will of the said Jean Key."

The jury found it proven that James M'Gregor had, with the aid of several people, forcibly carried off Jean Key. By a majority they found it not proven that Jean Key was privy or consenting to the design, but, at the same time, they unanimously found it proven, *for the alleviation of the panel's guilt in the premises*, that Jean Key did afterwards acquiesce in her condition. This finding was solely for the purpose of exempting the prisoner from capital punishment, but certain circumstances arose which brought about an unforeseen conclusion to the trial. On 20th November 1752 the advising of the case was to take place, but James M'Gregor did not make his appearance when called by a macer of Court, although upon the previous continuation he had been committed to the Tolbooth of Edinburgh by order of the Court. The magistrates of Edinburgh and the keeper of the Tolbooth were called, when it transpired that having in September received anonymous letters acquainting them that M'Gregor's escape from the Tolbooth, either by force or fraud, was intended, the magistrates made application to the Lord Justice-Clerk, then on his circuit at Ayr, for a warrant for having the prisoner carried from the Tolbooth to the Castle of Edinburgh, for his more safe and sure custody. The warrant having been obtained, James was handed over to a party of the City Guard, who conducted him to the Castle, and delivered him over to the Deputy-Governor, who informed the chief magistrage that the prisoner had escaped on the 16th inst. (November). Warrant was now granted for M'Gregor's apprehension, and the solicitors for the Crown were instructed to enquire into the manner in which he had escaped from the Castle. In the *Scots Magazine* for November 1752 the following particulars are given regarding the matter:—

"James M'Gregor, *alias* Drummond, under trial for carrying off Jean Key of Edinbelly, made his escape from Edinburgh Castle on the 16th. The manner of it is thus related:—In the evening he dressed himself in an old tattered big coat put over his own clothes, an old night cap, an old leather apron, and old dirty shoes and stockings, so as to personate a cobbler. When he was thus equipped, his daughter, a servant maid who assisted, and who was the only person with him in the room, except two of his young children, scolded the cobbler for having done his work carelessly, and this with such an audible voice as to be heard by the sentinels without the room door. About seven o'clock, while she was scolding, the pretended cobbler opened the room door, and went out with a pair of old shoes in his hand, muttering his discontent for the harsh usage he had received. He passed the guards unsuspected; but was soon missed, and a strict search made in the Castle, and also in the city, but all in vain. The sergeant, and some of the soldiers on duty, were put under confinement. On the 20th, the Court of Justiciary met to judge of the import of the verdict returned against him, and continued the diet till the 18th of December. We are told that the Commissioners of the Customs, in consequence of an application made to them, despatched orders to their officers fer strictly searching all ships outward bound, to prevent his escape out of the kingdom.

"*P.S.*—A Court-martial sat down in the Castle, December 8, in consequence, it is said, of orders from above, to inquire into this affair. It consisted of one lieutenant-colonel, two majors, and ten captains. They rose on the 13th. Two lieutenants and four private men were put under arrest; but we have not yet learned what is to be the result of their proceedings."

The same magazine in a subsequent number published the following :—

"A return from London to the report of the proceedings of the court-martial appointed to inquire into the manner of James Drummond's escape, arrived at Edinburgh, December 30. In consequence of which, two lieutenants, who commanded the guard the night Drummond escaped, are broke; the sergeant, who had the charge of locking the prisoner in his room, is reduced to a private man; the porter has been whipped, and all the rest are released."

Rob Oig.

I.

From Drunkie in the Highlands,
With four-and-twenty men,
Rob Oig is cam, a lady fair,
To carry from the plain.

II.

Glengyle and James with him are cam,
  To steal Jean Mitchell's dauchter,
And they have borne her far away,
  To haud his house in order.

III.

And he has ta'en Jean Key's white hand,
  And torn her grass-green sleeve,
And rudely tyed her on his horse,
  At her friends asked nae leave.

IV.

They rode till they cam to Ballyshine,
  At Ballyshine they tarried,
Nae time he gave her to be dressed,
  In cotton gown her married.

V.

Three held her up before the priest,
  Four carried her to bed, O !
Wi' wat'ry eyes, and mournfu' sighs,
  She in bed wi' Rob was laid, O !

VI.

" Haud far awa' from me, Rob Oig,
  " Haud far awa' from me,
" Before I lose my maidenhead,*
  " I'll try my strength with thee."

VII.

He's torn the cap from off her head,
  And thrown it to the way,
But ere she lost her maidenhead,
  She fought with him till day.

---

* The fact that Jean was a widow seems here to have been entirely lost sight of.

VIII.

" Wae fa', Rob Oig, upon your head,
  " For you have ravished me,
" And taen from me my maidenhead !
  " O ! would that I could dee."

IX.

" My father he is Rob Roy called,
  " And he has cows and ewes,
" And you are now my wedded wife,
  " And can nae longer chuse."

WILLY AND MARY.

I believe the following Jacobite song has never been correctly printed, a version differing in many important particulars from the present was privately printed some 40 years ago. It had been taken down from the mouth of an old cotter; the present edition is from an unique (as I consider it) broadsheet of the period. It is clearly a violent attack on William and Mary.

𝔚𝔦𝔩𝔩𝔶 𝔞𝔫𝔡 𝔐𝔞𝔯𝔶.

I.

Says Willy, " My uncle I'll beat,
 " Though I know it's unseemly and mean."
Says Mary, " My brother's a cheat,
 " And besides he's the son of a quean.
" We'll banish religion and truth,
 " For virtue's no friend in our case,
" But still we'll take care, in good sooth,
 " To wear a mask over our face."

(Chorus) Says Willy, " A king will I be."
    Says Mary, " A queen's crown for me."
    " My dady," said she,
    " My uncle," said he,
    " We'll send far away o'er the sea."

98

II.

" The traiterous party that murdered
  " Our grandfather, we will uphold,
" They shall be rewarded and honoured,
  " For that his sone they have sold.
" Thanks be to all knaves and queans,
  " Thanks to Presbitry and Treason,
" For these be the sanctified means
  " Which gain'd us a crown in good season.
(Chorus)   Says Willy, &c.

III.

" Blessed be those Independants
  " That took off our grandfather's head."
  Says Willy, " I'll have some descendants
  " Even if Mary dishonour my bed ;
" I care not who hatches the egg,
  " Nor how many others possess her,
" Her consent, there'll be no need to beg,
  " For she's willing enough for't, God bless her ! "
(Chorus)   Says Willy, &c.

IV.

  Says Mary, " Our father we'll honour,
  " Though we care not for splendour or pelf,
" Before that a crown hurts his head,
  " I'll dethrone him and wear it myself ;
" For he is now old and weak,
  " And while the sun shines we'll make hay,
" Our joy in this world we will seek,
  " For the devil will have us some day.

(Chorus)   Says good old Jamie, the king,
         " To honour and truth we will cling,
         " The heir of the crown,
         "Though deprived of his own,
         " Of Britain shall yet be the king."

www.ingramcontent.com/pod-product-compliance
Lightning Source LLC
Chambersburg PA
CBHW020626260626
47157CB00009B/3194